Victor Vicuna's Volcano Vacation

by Barbara deRubertis • illustrated by R.W. Alley

THE KANE PRESS / NEW YORK

Alpha Betty's Class

Alexander Anteater

Bobby Baboon

Corky Cub

Dilly Dog

Eddie Elephant

Frances Frog

Gertie Gorilla

Hanna Hippo

Lana Llama

Izzy Impala

Jeremy Jackrabbit

Kylie Kangaroo

Maxwell Moose

Library of Congress Cataloging-in-Publication Data

deRubertis, Barbara.
Victor Vicuna's volcano vacation / by Barbara deRubertis ; illustrated by R.W. Alley.
p. cm. — (Animal antics A to Z)
Summary: Victor Vicuna is nervous about his vacation to Verna Aardvark's Volcano Village,
and Verna's pet raven makes him even more nervous.
ISBN 978-1-57565-355-6 (library binding : alk. paper) — ISBN 978-1-57565-347-1 (pbk. : alk. paper) —
ISBN 978-1-57565-386-0 (e-book) *5152 8700*
[1. Volcanoes—Fiction. 2. Fear—Fiction. 3. Ravens—Fiction. 4. Animals—Fiction. 5. Alphabet.]
I. Alley, R. W. (Robert W.), ill. II. Title.
PZ7.D4475Vi 2011
[E]—dc22   2010051321

1 3 5 7 9 10 8 6 4 2

First published in the United States of America in 2011 by Kane Press, Inc.
Printed in the United States of America
WOZ0711

Series Editor: Juliana Hanford
Book Design: Edward Miller

Animal Antics A to Z is a registered trademark of Kane Press, Inc.

www.kanepress.com

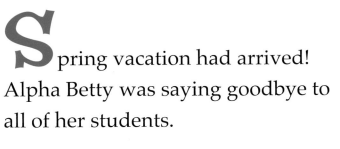

Spring vacation had arrived! Alpha Betty was saying goodbye to all of her students.

Victor Vicuna's parents waved from their van. "It's time to leave, Victor! We have a long drive ahead of us!"

"Now don't worry, Victor," said Alpha Betty. "You'll have a *lovely* vacation!"

Victor's family was going to Verna's Volcano Village. And Victor's vivid imagination was making him nervous!

Verna Aardvark advertised: "Seven heavenly cabins on Shiver River!"

Victor imagined a freezing cold river with heaving chunks of ice.

Verna's ad also said: "Visit Vampire Cave!"

Victor imagined a cave filled with *vampire bats*!

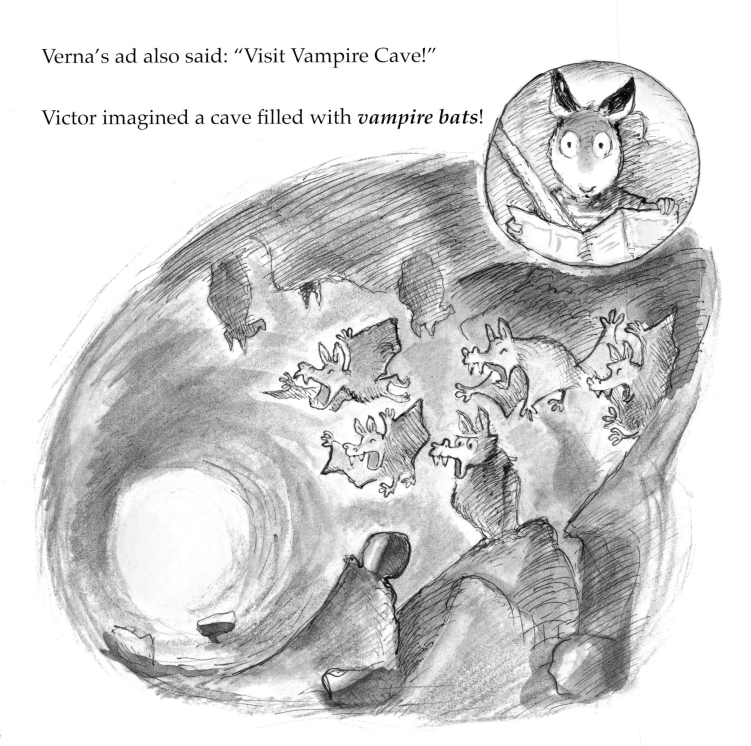

Then the ad said: "See a marvelous view of Stove-Top Volcano!"

Victor imagined a big volcano spewing rivers of red hot lava!

Verna added: "Our pet raven will welcome you when you arrive!"

Victor had visions of a large, scary bird with a loud, screechy voice!

Victor's family finally arrived at Verna's
Volcano Village.

Immediately, a huge raven swooped down!
"Caw! Caw!" it screeched.
Victor covered his head. "Go away!" he shouted.

Verna Aardvark came running.
"Don't be afraid! This is our pet raven.
Her name is Nevva Moore."

Victor stared at Nevva nervously.

Verna took Victor's family to their cabin.
Nevva Moore hovered over Victor.

"You can leave now, Nevva!" Victor whispered.
"Please!"

The next morning, Victor's family set out on their first adventure.

They walked down a weaving path to Shiver River.
Gentle waves splashed on the rocks.
There were *no* heaving chunks of ice.

Victor ventured out onto some rocks.

Suddenly, Nevva Moore dove down beside him.
Victor ducked. Then . . . *VOOOSH!*
He slipped into the chilly river!

"Help!" Victor cried. "Save me!"

Dad grabbed Victor's life vest.
Then his parents heaved him ashore.

Dad carried a shivering, quivering Victor back
to the cabin.

Nevva hovered behind them.

"G-g-go away, Nevva," Victor said.
"You made me fall in the river!"

"Maybe Nevva was just trying to warn you
about the slippery rocks," said Mom.

"Maybe . . . ," thought Victor. "But maybe not!"

The next day, Victor's parents planned another adventure . . . to Vampire Cave.

Nevva followed them *again*.

Nevva led the way through a dark tunnel and into a vast cavern.

It was like a fairyland!

Then Victor looked up. Dark creatures hung from the ceiling, slowly moving their wings.

"VAMPIRE BATS!" screamed Victor.

The bats started flying wildly around the cavern. Nevva dove down and hovered over Victor.

Frantically, Victor ran out of the cave . . .
and all the way back to the cabin.

Nevva Moore flew right behind him.

Soon Mom and Dad arrived. They said,
"Those were NOT vampire bats, Victor.
And Nevva was probably just trying to protect you."

"I don't know," Victor said in a low voice.
"I think Nevva may be a vampire raven!"

On the third day, Victor's parents planned
a visit to Stove-Top Volcano. Visions of
red hot lava filled Victor's imagination.

"I vote against visiting Stove-Top," Victor said.
But Mom and Dad out-voted him.

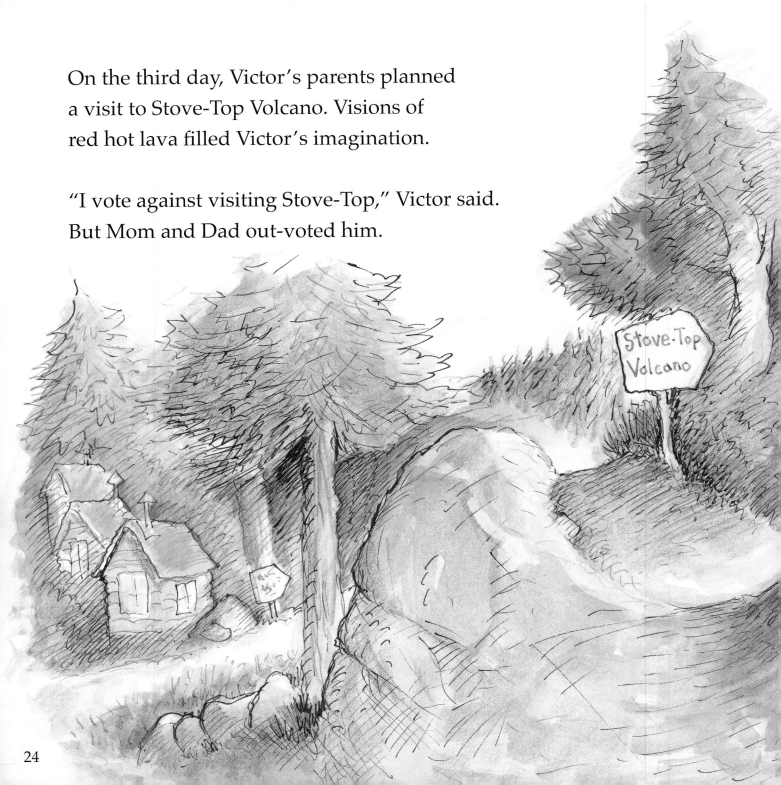

Stove-Top
Volcano

Victor and his parents hiked to the top of the
volcano. Of course, Nevva followed them.

They all admired the lovely view of the
volcano's crater.

Suddenly, Nevva began acting nervous.
She waved her wings. She cawed loudly.
And she started hopping down the trail.

Then she turned and stared at Victor.
Victor stared back.

And he began to wonder. . . .

Stove-Top
Volcano

Was Nevva trying to warn him about something?
What if she wasn't a vampire raven?
What if she really *was* trying to protect him?

Quickly, Victor turned to his parents.
"Mom! Dad! I think we should follow Nevva!"

Nevva flew just ahead of Victor and his parents.
As they ran, the ground began to vibrate.
A plume of vapor curled up from the crater.

Victor had never run so fast!

The signs read:
Verna's Volcano Village
Stove-Top Volcano

By the time they reached Verna's village,
the volcano was quiet again.

"Old Stove-Top was showing off for you today,"
Verna said. "Sometimes our volcano likes to
rumble and grumble . . . and vent a little vapor.
Nevva can sense when that's about to happen!"

Victor smiled. He sat down beside Nevva. "You really *were* trying to keep me safe from the rocks . . . and the bats . . . and the volcano! Thank you, Nevva!"

And Nevva said, *"Caw!"*

When spring vacation was over, Victor brought his *favorite* photo to school.

Of course, it was a photo of Victor Vicuna and his new friend—that clever raven, Nevva Moore!

Victor Vicuna and Nevva Moore

FUN FACTS

- Home: Vicunas live mainly in wild herds high in the Andes Mountains of South America.
- Family: The vicuna is the smallest member of the camel family. Because vicunas were hunted too much, they are now protected as an endangered species.
- Appearance: Vicunas have coats of long, thick, silky wool that protect them from freezing temperatures.
- **Did You Know?** Vicunas communicate in *many* interesting ways! A high-pitched whinny warns of danger. Guttural sounds announce anger or fear. And a soft humming sound is a friendly greeting!

LOOK BACK

Learning to identify letter sounds (phonemes) at the beginning, middle, and end of words is called "phonemic awareness."

- The word *van* <u>starts</u> with the *v* sound. Listen to the words on page 29 being read again. When you hear a word that <u>starts</u> with the *v* sound, make a "v" with two fingers on each hand and say the word.
- The word *river* <u>has</u> the *v* sound in the middle of the word. Listen to the words on page 31 being read again. When you hear a word that has the *v* sound in the <u>middle</u>, repeat the word slowly. Put both arms in the air in a giant V shape when you come to the *v* sound.
- **Challenge:** The word *wave* has the *v* sound at the <u>end</u>. Change the beginning *w* to *c*. What word have you made? Now change the *c* to *g*, *p*, *r*, and *s*.

TRY THIS!

Listen carefully as each word in the word bank below is read aloud slowly.

- If the word <u>begins</u> with the *v* sound, place your hands on top of your head and then lift them like an erupting *volcano* while you say the word!
- If the word has the *v* sound in the <u>middle</u>, tuck your hands under your arms and flap your wings like a *raven* while you say the word!

volcano raven seven van vacation
river village lava over visit cover
shiver hover view vest voice

FOR MORE ACTIVITIES, go to Victor Vicuna's website: www.kanepress.com/AnimalAntics/VictorVicuna.html
You'll also find a recipe for Victor Vicuna's Veggie Pie!